Aladdin and the Genies

Written by Vivian French

Illustrated by Victoria Assanelli

Collins

Chapter 1

WANTED! Clever young boy who wants to be rich!
Must be willing to obey orders without asking questions.
If interested, knock on the blue door in the street
of camels.

Signed: Kadar Ghazi the merchant

The notice was pinned on the town gate. Aladdin read it carefully. "I want to be rich," he said. "And I don't ask many questions."

"Yes, you do," said his mother. "You're always asking questions!"

"I can pretend I don't," Aladdin told her. "And then we can afford some food. I'm starving!"

His mother shook her head. "We don't know anything about this Kadar Ghazi."

"Don't worry," Aladdin said. "I'm very clever, remember!"

His mother sighed. "Be careful."

Chapter 2

Trying not to feel too hopeful, Aladdin soon found the blue door. He knocked, and the door opened ... but there was nobody there.

Aladdin strode inside. The room was dark and empty. There were no cushions and no rugs ... just a bare stone floor. Wondering what would happen next, he decided to wait for a while.

"Aren't you afraid?" a deep voice echoed around the room.

"No," Aladdin said. "I can't see anything to be afraid of."

"Good!" said the voice. A door in the wall swung open, and an enormous man dressed in shimmering silk appeared.

"He looks extremely wealthy," Aladdin thought.

"I'm Kadar Ghazi," the man growled. "Who are you?"

Aladdin bowed. "My name is Aladdin. I don't ask questions, and I want to be rich."

"Excellent! Then this is for you." Kadar Ghazi handed Aladdin a gold ring, and Aladdin put it on his finger.

"Hold my coat, and shut your eyes!"
the merchant ordered.

Chapter 3

Doing his best to look cool and calm, Aladdin did as
he was told. When he opened his eyes he was standing
in a hot, dusty desert. In front of him was the opening
to a cave.

"H'm," he thought. "This man seems to be a magician,
not a merchant." But he said nothing and waited
for his next order.

Kadar Ghazi pointed to the narrow opening.
"Fetch the oil lamp you'll find inside. It belongs
to me – but I'm too big to reach it!"

"Yes, sir." Aladdin squeezed into the cave, wriggling his way between the rocky walls until he reached the end … and there was an old oil lamp.

"Have you got it, boy?" Kadar Ghazi sounded impatient. "Quick! Give it to me!"

Aladdin looked at the dented and dusty lamp, and scratched his head. "There's something strange happening here," he thought, and he called out, "Why do you want it so much?"

"I said, no questions! Just bring me the lamp!"

Aladdin knelt down in the cold, clammy darkness. "Not until you tell me why you want it."

A furious roar echoed round the cave. "You miserable toad of a boy! You worm! I'll shut you in here forever!"

And with a mighty CRASH, a gigantic boulder fell across the entrance.

Chapter 4

It was pitch-black now – so dark Aladdin couldn't see his hand in front of his face. His heart was thumping hard, but he took a deep breath. "Perhaps there's another way out? Brrrrr! It's freezing!" He shivered, and rubbed his hands together to warm them ...

And a cloud of green smoke filled the cave.

"Good afternoon, master." A small figure bowed deeply to Aladdin. "I'm the genie of the ring, and your wish is my command. Where would you like to go?"

Blinking in surprise, Aladdin pinched himself. "Are you real?" he asked.

The genie frowned. "Of course, master. Now, what is your wish?"

"I wish I was at home, with an enormous bowl of soup," Aladdin said.

"Soup I can't provide." The genie bowed again. "I'm only the genie of journeys. Different genies have different powers, but I can take you to your house."

Chapter 5

Green smoke swirled around Aladdin, and the next minute he found himself in his kitchen. He gazed at the familiar room in astonishment. How had the genie done that?

His mother ran to hug him. "Did the merchant pay you? Are you rich?"

Aladdin shook his head, pulled the dusty old lamp from his pocket and explained what had happened.

His mother was horrified, but she took the lamp. "I'll polish this," she said. "Perhaps we can sell it." She rubbed at the lamp with her shawl and …

There was a huge flash, and another genie appeared in a cloud of purple smoke. He was ten times the size of the genie of the ring, and dressed in shining silver.

"What's your wish?"

Aladdin wasn't afraid, even though the genie towered above him. "Who are you?" he asked.

The genie bowed. "I'm the genie of the lamp, master. Your wish is my command."

"Really?" Aladdin folded his arms. "Can you bring us some money?"

"Of course, master," the genie said, and waved his hand. An old clay pot on the windowsill tipped over, and a heap of gold coins tumbled out.

"WOW!" Aladdin said, staring at the money. "That's amazing! What else can you do?"

The genie shrugged. "Whatever you wish, master." And he disappeared in a swirl of purple smoke.

"Goodness me!" Aladdin's mother's eyes widened. "A magic lamp!"

Aladdin nodded, grabbed her hands and danced her round the room. "We're rich, Mother! Rich!"

Chapter 6

From then on, Aladdin and his mother had no worries. If they needed anything, they simply rubbed the magic lamp, and the genie brought it. They might have lived happily ever after ... but one day, as Aladdin was walking in the town, a golden carriage trundled past.

Aladdin recognised it as the sultan's coach. Looking inside, he saw Princess Lily Flower, and his heart missed a beat.

The young man bowed low. "Princess," he said, "I'll be your servant for ever and for always. You're more beautiful than the sun and the moon and the stars, and I love you ..."

The princess laughed. "Show me a rose-pink swan and a sky-blue nightingale, and I'll love you too!"

The carriage rattled away, and Aladdin wandered home in a dream.

Chapter 7

That night, Aladdin rubbed the lamp. "Bring me the finest jewels," he ordered the genie, "the most beautiful clothes for my mother and a splendid carriage for her to ride in."

The genie waved a hand. "It's done, master."

The jewels shone like the sun. Aladdin heaped them into baskets, and put them in the carriage.

"Mother," he said. "You must take these to the sultan. Tell him your son is a prince. Tell him I have a palace of snow-white marble, and a lake where rose-pink swans swim round a crystal island. Tell him I have a grove of silver trees where sky-blue nightingales sing all night and all day. And ask him if he'll permit your son, Prince Aladdin, to marry Princess Lily Flower."

His mother stared at him. "But, Aladdin! You've none of those things!"

Aladdin picked up the magic lamp, and winked. "By the time you come home, I'll have them all!"

The sultan gazed in delighted astonishment at the deep red rubies and the sparkling diamonds, and he listened carefully as Aladdin's mother told him and Princess Lily Flower about the marble palace.

"Rose-pink swans?" the princess asked. "And sky-blue nightingales? This must be the handsome young man I saw today! Father – let me marry this prince!"

The sultan let a trickle of sea-green emeralds run through his fingers. "It shall be as you wish, my daughter."

Chapter 8

The wedding was the talk of the country, and Aladdin's snow-white marble palace was declared the most wonderful sight in the east. Its fame spread far and wide, and so did tales of the handsome Prince Aladdin and his lovely wife, Princess Lily Flower. These tales crossed the sea and reached the ears of the magician, Kadar Ghazi.

His eyes blazed. "So the little worm escaped! And not only has he escaped, but he's using MY magic lamp!" Scowling, the magician sat down to think. At last he nodded. "I have a plan! Soon that lamp will be MINE!"

While the magician was plotting and planning, Princess Lily Flower was as happy as the sky-blue nightingales … apart from one thing. She loved Aladdin dearly, but she couldn't understand why a dented old lamp was his most precious possession. When she asked, he just blew her a kiss and told her not to worry about it, but the princess was still puzzled. Everything else they owned was new and sparkling …

Chapter 9

One morning, Aladdin left in a carriage to bring Lily Flower's father, the sultan, back for a visit. That same day, a lamp seller came riding up to the palace calling, "New lamps for old! New lamps for old!" and the princess clapped her hands in delight. She'd give the lamp seller the old lamp, and surprise Aladdin with a shining new one on his return.

The lamp seller hunched over a stick, and Princess Lily Flower couldn't see his face. His hand trembled as he reached out for Aladdin's lamp. "You make an old man very happy, Princess," he said in a husky voice, and Lily Flower smiled at him.

"Poor man. You won't ever be rich if you exchange new things for old!"

"Oh, but I will!" The man's voice changed completely as he snatched the lamp. He stood up straight, threw back his old robe, and laughed a loud and terrible laugh. "I'm the great Kadar Ghazi, and I'll be as rich as your darling Aladdin ... and all that he has will be mine, mine, MINE!"

He turned his back on the horrified princess, and rubbed the lamp. Lily Flower gasped as the genie of the lamp appeared in billowing clouds of purple.

"Take it all away!" Kadar Ghazi ordered. "All that is here, all you have created – take it to my land across the sea!"

"Your wish is my command." The genie waved his hand, and the princess, the palace, the lake, the rose-pink swans and the sky-blue nightingales were whirled up into clouds of purple smoke.

29

Chapter 10

When Aladdin returned with the sultan, he stared and stared. It was as if his marble palace had never existed – all he could see was sand.

The sultan scrambled out of the golden carriage, tripping over his robes in his hurry. "Sorcery! Wizards!" he shouted. "They've taken my daughter!" He turned to Aladdin. "Listen to me, young man! If she's not back in 40 days, your head will roll!" He climbed back into the carriage. "Take me home! This place stinks of bad magic!"

As the carriage drove away, Aladdin clenched his fists. Who could have done this? Then he noticed the footprints in the sand.

"H'm," he said to himself. "Footprints going one way – but not going back! It must be that wicked magician! But what can I do without the lamp? Will I ever see my darling Lily Flower again?" He wiped away a tear. As he did so, the ring on his finger caught his eye.

"Of course! The genie of journeys!" Aladdin rubbed the ring, and at once the genie appeared in a puff of green smoke.

"Thought you'd forgotten about me, master," he said. "What's your wish?"

"I want to be standing beside the Princess Lily Flower," Aladdin told him.

Chapter 11

In the blink of an eye, Aladdin found himself beside the princess at the top of the marble palace tower.

"Dearest Aladdin! I knew you'd find me!" She hugged him tightly. "That horrible magician! He says he'll never let me go!"

"We'll see about that. We need to trick Kadar Ghazi somehow. Can you think of how we can get the magic lamp back?"

Lily Flower frowned. "You never told me it was magic. I'd never have given it away if I'd known."

Aladdin hung his head. "I'm sorry. You're right … from now on, I promise I'll tell you everything."

At the sound of heavy footsteps on the stairs,
Aladdin hid behind a pillar.

Kadar Ghazi stamped towards the princess, with
a greasy smile. "So, my pretty little pigeon! Have you
decided? You'll never see that worm of a boy again,
so now you can be MY wife!"

Princess Lily Flower gave him a smile as sweet as sugar. "Dear Kadar Ghazi, you must be the most powerful of magicians to bring me here. Is there anything you can't do?" She tilted her head to one side. "May I have a string of pearls to wear when we are married?"

The magician's smile grew wider. "Just give me a moment, my pigeon, and the pearls will be yours."

The princess pouted. "But I want to see you working your magic! Do it now, or I'll change my mind!"

Kadar Ghazi hesitated, and the princess gave a little laugh. "I see! You can't do it!"

"Yes, I can!" The magician pulled the lamp from his pocket. "Watch!"

"Oooh ..." The princess leant forward. "What's that? May I see?"

"NO!" Kadar Ghazi clasped the magic lamp to his chest.

Princess Lily Flower frowned. "But if I'm to be your wife, we should share everything. Please?"

The magician hesitated a second time, then placed the lamp in her outstretched hands. She smiled sweetly once more, then spun round and tossed the lamp to Aladdin. As soon as he caught it, he rubbed it.

Kadar Ghazi gave a furious roar, but he was too late …

The tower filled with purple smoke as the genie of the lamp bowed to Aladdin. "Yes, master?"

"Take me, my palace and my oh! so clever princess home," Aladdin ordered, "but make sure you leave this evil man behind. Do as I say, and I'll set you free!"

The genie bowed very low. "Thank you, master. It shall be as you wish."

41

Purple smoke whirled and swirled and darkened the air. When it faded away, Aladdin and Princess Lily Flower were still standing on the top of the tower … and in the distance was Aladdin's home town. There was no sign of the terrible Kadar Ghazi.

Chapter 12

"We're back," Aladdin sighed with relief, and he kissed Lily Flower.

"Yes," she said. "And now we can be happy ... but promise me one thing!"

"Anything, my princess."

"No more secrets. And no more wishes!"

"I promise." Aladdin pulled the ring from his finger. "Go free, genie of journeys!"

There was a puff of green smoke, and a voice said, "Thank you, master!"

Aladdin looked fondly at the lamp in his hands, rubbed it one last time and tossed it in the air.
A wisp of purple drifted down as it soared up into the clear blue sky ... and disappeared.

"Thank you, master," came the genie's voice.
"You've given me freedom and happiness. I wish
the same to you and Princess Lily Flower ...
and now, farewell for ever!"

Aladdin's wishes

47

Ideas for reading

Written by Clare Dowdall, PhD
Lecturer and Primary Literacy Consultant

Reading objectives:
- identify themes and conventions
- discuss words and phrases that capture the reader's interest and imagination
- draw inferences and justify these with evidence

Spoken language objectives:
- participate in discussions, presentations, performances, role-play, improvisations and debates

Curriculum links: PSHE

Resources: paper and pencils for note making, ICT, drawing materials

Build a context for reading

- Read the title and look at the illustration. Ask children to explain what a genie is and where they come from.
- Read the blurb together. Ask children what Aladdin had wished for and what they'd wish for if they found a genie who would grant wishes.
- Discuss what happens in well-known versions of this traditonal tale. Ask for information about characters, settings and events.

Understand and apply reading strategies

- Turn to pp2–3 and read the opening of the story aloud. Discuss what makes this a good story opening, and how it differs from usual fairy story openings. Focus on how the author uses language to create interest.
- Look at the sentence *"Must be willing to obey orders without asking questions."* Discuss how this makes the reader feel about Kadar Ghazi. Begin to create lists of vocabulary to describe Aladdin and Kadar Ghazi.